Undercurrent

A Waterlore Romance

Riona Beck

Undine PRESS

Undercurrent: A Waterlore Romance
Copyright ©2024 by Riona Beck.

All rights reserved. No portion of this book may be reproduced, distributed, or transmitted in any form or by any electronic or mechanical means, including information storage and retrieval systems, without written permission from the publisher or author, except for the use of brief quotations in a book review and certain other noncommercial use permitted by U.S. copyright law. This book is a work of fiction. Resemblance to actual persons and things living or dead, locales, or events is entirely coincidental.

Published by: Undine Press
Character design by: Dawn Davidson
Cover design by: Riona Beck

Dedication

For those of you who love the sea and its mysteries.

Table of Contents

Dedication	*3*
Chapter 1	*5*
Chapter 2	*11*
Chapter 3	*22*
Chapter 4	*29*
Chapter 5	*40*
Chapter 6	*49*
Chapter 7	*60*
Thank You	*65*
More from Riona Beck	*67*
About the Author	*68*

Chapter 1

The last thing Mirren expected to find after the storm, on her corner of the island or anywhere, was a naked man.

The wind had howled all night, driving waves upon the shore and battering her little bothy. She had slept little and fitfully.

When morning broke grey and the storm ceased, she rose early, gathered her wide basket, and took the little path down to the shoreline to look for seaweed. No one would be about yet—or so she thought. She'd scarcely begun to peel the heavy, broad strips washed up from the depths when she discovered that someone was there after all. Not a fisherman, for there were no boats. And fishermen, as a general rule, did not go about their business without their clothes on.

He stood waist deep in the frigid grey water, facing the horizon with his back to her.

No one in their right mind wanders into the sea without a stitch of clothes, especially not at the tail end of winter.

Mirren paused on the beach. He hadn't seen her, and didn't seem to hear her, either. Upon further inspection, the man looked strong and uninjured. Dark, wet hair hung past his naked shoulders and grazed a lean, equally naked back that tapered into a narrow waist just visible above the gentle, rippling waves.

Mirren was not a complete innocent. The male form was not a total mystery to her. Yet she wasn't prepared for the interest and heat that bloomed within her at the sight of him.

She tossed her curly brown hair over her shoulder. *Don't be silly,* she scolded herself. *He's likely got himself a wife. Or a missing tooth, or an over-fondness for ale. Or he's lost his clothes gambling the night away.*

He turned around and caught her gaze. His eyes were as grey as the sea, an undercurrent of something wild and tantalizing shadowing their depths. His frame was slender, not large, and his chest and abdomen were as lean as his back, suggesting he was familiar with a hard life. Everyone on the island was familiar with hard living. But Mirren didn't recognize him from the village. By the grin that spread across his face, she could see that all his teeth were perfectly intact, neat and healthy—and that he was a man who liked an appreciative gaze.

And I am someone who likes to make the first move.

"It's early for bathing," she called. "Have you lost something? A wager, perhaps, or your wits?"

His grin broadened into a smile that dimpled one cheek. "I've never found the need for a wager," he replied. His voice was low yet carried easily over the incessant rush of the waves. "My wits are sound as ever, whatever that's worth." He stumbled sideways as a larger wave crashed against him, both covering and threatening to reveal.

Mirren found herself at the water's edge as a new, distressing thought came to her. "You haven't come in on the storm, have you? A shipwreck?" She craned her neck to look along the expanse of the beach, but saw no signs of flotsam anywhere. If he'd been washed ashore, surely there would be signs.

"No, I've come to no harm, lass. But I am a newcomer of sorts. And I find myself lacking the essentials." The dimple returned as his smile turned sheepish, somehow making him even more attractive.

"You'll catch cold if you stay in there. Take this." She pulled off her shawl and held it out, watching in fascination as he strode towards her, muscles rippling with the effort. She stumbled backwards as he reached the sand. Water streamed down his skin, smooth as finely carved stone. As he took the shawl, his fingers brushed hers with a jolt that made Mirren drop her gaze, where she had a fine view of the stranger as he wrapped the material around his waist.

"Lacking the essentials, indeed," she repeated breathlessly, and cleared her throat. "What will your wife say to this foolishness?"

"I'll have to ask her when I meet her."

A smirk tugged at Mirren's mouth. Oh, he was smooth. Far more so than the men of the village. Every unwed male from eighteen to fifty-eight had offered her marriage after her brother's death, claiming how wrong it was for her to live alone. This had made her want to keep her solitary life all the more. The work was hard, but she was harder, and as stubborn as the sea. She'd had two or three brief dalliances, giving her more experience than many a maiden carried with her to the marriage bed. But not one man had ever tempted her to settle down. Each had parted ways once he knew she would not make the wife he wanted, acting as though they'd never shared more than a chaste, everyday interaction. Mirren was content to leave these facades unchallenged.

But this stranger was different with his haunting, sea-grey eyes that never left her face. He was alluring and possibly dangerous. And Mirren, who had lived her entire life by the sea and knew its moods, its generosity and mercilessness, had never met anyone who seemed to hold all these things the way this man did. It pulled at her like the tide and sent a thrill of arousal through her. *Steady, girl,* she warned herself. *A little fun never hurt anyone,* herself warned back. *Oh no, but ruthless men and pregnancy might*. She bit back a scoff at herself. Sometimes her practical side was far too bossy for her liking.

"I'd be grateful for any clothes, if you can spare them." The stranger broke into her muddled thoughts. "Unless you have men folk who'd object."

The idea made her laugh. Mirren narrowed her eyes. "Plenty of men would object, but I pay them no mind. I'll not leave a stranger without hospitality. You'll have clothes and food at my place. But you mind this: try one trick and you'll find out how handy I am with a knife."

"I don't doubt it," he replied. "I'm grateful for the offer." Mirren felt his words in her chest, in her belly, reminding her suddenly that he stood a handbreadth away. Up close she could see the green and gold flecks in his grey eyes. She let her gaze trail down to the hollow in his throat, the smooth, hair-dusted chest. A silver chain hung there, so fine it could have been spun from spider's webs, and on it rested a charm whose shape she could not quite make out. She wanted to touch it, to remove it and feel the warmth of another's skin beneath her own hands. She wanted to run her hands down his torso and feel his firm length in her grip. Hunger flared dangerously hot, competing with warnings firing in her mind, as her gaze snapped up to find his eyes mirroring the heat she felt.

"And if you need anything in return," he continued, his voice a low burr, "you have only to ask."

Those eyes made her want to throw caution to the wind and ask for what she wanted. Or preferably show him, right there on the beach. But it was morning, and the fishermen would come to the beach soon. She didn't know this stranger at all. As alluring as this man was, if life had taught her anything, it was to keep caution nearby.

"Then we had better get you dressed," she said, shrugging one shoulder, "unless you want to be caught."

"Depends on who catches me."

"People will talk if they see you." *Not to mention, I'm not sure how many more risks my reputation can withstand.*

He cocked his head to one side, mock concern in his voice. "Is that a challenge?"

Mirren only laughed.

The stranger adjusted his grip on the shawl slung low on his hips. "Are you going to tell me what you want in return, or shall I guess?"

"That depends." Mirren leaned closer, tilting her chin up. "Are you going to tell me what you were looking for out there?"

His low, brief chuckle sent a thrill through her. "I'm hoping I've found it."

Mirren had no answer to that. She turned, expecting him to follow, and hauled the basket along with a smirk on her lips and heat pooling between her legs.

She had no idea who this stranger was, or what his intentions were. She was used to taking care of herself. She was used to getting what she wanted. *I want to know if he's as amenable to a day's dalliance as his anatomy suggests. But first, I'm going to test him.*

Chapter 2

Flynn kept his distance as he followed the young woman to her bothy. He didn't wish to set her on edge, scarce believing he'd finally met her face to face. She didn't know he had watched her for some time.

He'd lived a solitary life. It was the way of his kind, and it had never bothered him. While he had made forays into fishing villages once or twice before, it never lasted long. Until, that is, he saw a certain young woman on the beach.

Perhaps her own solitude had first caught his attention. According to his previous observations, humans clustered together, as if isolation were a curse. This human lived alone. She was wrestling seaweed from the beach the day he first saw her, a small, slim figure no match for the power of the ocean in which he swam and lived and devoured. Yet she went about her work with such determination. A borderline ferocity, even, as if the seaweed had much to answer for and she brought its reckoning. He returned every day to watch her from the shelter of the rocks. The more he answered the lure of curiosity and the more he witnessed her at work, the more she intrigued him. What made her so fearsome, this fragile slip of a human? What made her shun her own kind? And why was this pull towards her irrevocable?

Something unknown in him answered this pull. Something he wanted to understand. Something that compelled him to take his human form, and wander out, exposed, where she would see him, where he could meet her face to face—if she didn't run from him first.

And now he was walking behind her. He'd heard her voice, smelled the soap and salt on her skin, and she hadn't run. She'd invited him home, even. Meeting her brought a rush of sensations, some familiar, some not. He was awash with hunger for her, the human kind he'd experience before. But perhaps the strangest sensation of all was fear.

This woman was real, no longer a distant fantasy. She was vulnerable in her humanity, beneath her laughing, teasing capability, wary beneath her flirtations. For the first time, Flynn realized the precariousness of his situation. His actions could leave a mark on them both. It was a strange and sobering thought.

He had no expectations and a thousand desires. He wanted to know her thoughts, to catch a glimpse of the woman beneath her playful, evasive manners, if she would allow it. Any time spent in her presence was a gift more generous than anything the sea could ever give him.

She pushed the door open and let him inside. It was a small space, clean and sparse. A fireplace took up most of one wall. A bed and a trunk sat alongside another, the bed small and neatly made.

Flynn's thoughts rioted at the sight of it. The woman made a show of taking a slim knife from the kitchen and tucked it into her apron, smiling merrily at him, and his thoughts settled down with proper sobriety.

"You can put these on." She pulled a bundle of clothes from the trunk and handed them to him.

He thanked her. The small, intimate space of the bothy gave him pause. This was her domain, her safety, and she had invited him in. Even though she had seen him naked there was something different about dressing in front of her, in her home. He waited for the woman to turn around before dropping the shawl and struggling into the clothes. They were well-made if worn, and hung on his frame as if they had belonged to a larger man.

"Will your husband miss these clothes?" He asked. When she didn't turn around, Flynn ventured into her line of vision and repeated the question. His voice seemed to startle her out of a reverie. She blinked her large hazel eyes.

"They were my brother's. He died of illness. I am not married." Accepting the shawl from him, she retrieved two small, rough pieces of bread from a box and handed him one. "Eat up," she continued briskly. ""I'll need to gather as much seaweed as possible today. You could help me with that."

She was unmarried. He'd expected as much from his observations of her, but the relief he felt at hearing the affirmation was immeasurable. Just as great was the fact that she was giving him a chance to stay, at least for a few hours. "Would you consider us even if I helped you gather seaweed?" He asked playfully, very much hoping the answer would be no. "Clothes in exchange for work?"

She pursed her pretty lips, yet it didn't quite stop the grin tugging on her mouth. "Not quite. I gave you food, too. You could start by sharing your name."

"Flynn."

"Mirren."

"Mirren," Flynn repeated. Her name felt like a current on his tongue, one he could happily drown in. "I am sorry for your loss, Mirren, but glad I found your shore."

They carried baskets back to the water's edge and gathered seaweed, a simple enough task if a burdensome one. Flynn, awkward without the flirtations which came so easily to him, tried to make conversation. "How do you spend your days, Mirren of the shore?"

"Oh, general mischief and skullduggery." She tossed him a brief grin, then laughed at his bewildered expression. The sound sent a jolt of delight through him. "Just like this, really. Working." Bending over, she set the basket down next to a large tuft of dune grass and looked out to sea, a remote look stealing across her face. Strands of dark, curling hair escaped their knot and caressed her cheek and throat. He wanted to gently brush her hair away and cup her face and bring her to the present with a searing, searching kiss. But she didn't seem ready for that, not yet. "I'll have to take the boat out and fish tomorrow. If you're not adverse to that, I could use the help."

She looked at him with a questioning glance.

"I'm not adverse," he said, and grinned like a silly boy when she turned away and walked back towards the bothy, her hips swaying in a way that drove him mad. *She wants me to stay.* It was too good to be true.

He walked at her side this time, thinking it would be strange to follow her like a lost puppy now that they'd exchanged names. For all the desire he'd seen in her eyes, Flynn admitted to himself that he felt nervous. What if he moved too fast and scared her away? Another thought struck him, terrible and unwanted: she didn't know what he really was. He feared what would happen if she found out.

The thought receded when Mirren, picking up her pace, cast him a glance over her shoulder. Flynn could have sworn he saw that tormenting smile of hers tugging one corner of her mouth, making her look mischievous.

She showed him how to dry the morning's finds in long, wavy-edged rows of slippery ribbons on low rock walls shaded by thatch. Kelp ricks, Mirren called them. He didn't care what they were called when they provided the chance to work so closely that he couldn't avoid softly bumping into her. She must have noticed, for that tiny smile lurked in the corners of her mouth, but she said nothing.

The long grasses rustled in the wind, brushing against his legs and bare feet. He had insisted that he fared better without shoes. Which was just as well, as Mirren had sold everything of her brothers' save what Flynn wore.

They stood on the low, wind-swept dunes near her bothy, overlooking the vast sea on one side. Farmland stretched in the other direction, dotted with red-haired cows huddling together on the low, rolling hills. In the distance he could see another stretch of the beach, and near that, a cluster of buildings that must be the village. He'd only been there a few times before. Overhead, seagulls wheeled and screeched.

"It's a lonely place for one person," he said.

"I'm used to it," Mirren replied, bent over the last of the seaweed. She straightened and looked up at him, her eyes piercing. "I have questions, Flynn."

Of course she would. *I should have anticipated them.* She would be curious, and he would have to answer her honestly–as honestly as possible. He maintained a calm expression as he replied, "ask me."

"Are you in trouble with someone? The law?"

"No. Neither." He exhaled; that much was true. None of his kind cared whether he lived or died.

"You haven't left a sweetheart behind? No pretty girl crying her eyes out for want of you?"

"No." He had dallied with a barmaid a few times, and was delighted to find that at least one human woman found him desirable, even if she did end their encounters before he was ready. Not long after, he'd seen Mirren. Flynn silently thanked the barmaid for so generously educating and releasing him.

"Hm." Mirren's fists rested on her hips. She studied him openly, without cynicism. "Why are you here, Flynn?"

He ran a hand through his hair, thinking frantically. *You. You are the reason I'm here*. That did not seem like an answer that would put him in a favorable light, honest though it was. He thought of all the human behaviors he'd observed during the past few months. It was fascinating, and sometimes confusing, to witness the subtleties and nuances in manner and speech. Speech, especially. Humans seemed to say one thing and mean another. With that thought, an answer came to him.

"I want a fresh start," he said. That was true, even if it was not the whole truth, even if he had not allowed himself to think of what might come after that start.

"Are you a good man, Flynn?"

By the deep, how was he supposed to answer that? He suddenly envied the seaweed that Mirren wrestled from the shore: it didn't have to withstand such questioning. He could feel his calm expression falter under her scrutiny. Yet how could he look away? Her mouth twitched with humor, as if she enjoyed watching him squirm. But her eyes were serious as death.

Something tugged within his chest. *How can I disappoint her? She will be my undoing.*

If she was a tide, he was near drowning, and he could almost give himself up for lost.

"I don't know, Mirren," he answered. "I don't know if I'm a good man."

"Hm." Mirren dropped her hands and stepped closer so that they stood a hand's breadth away, her gaze searching, searing. "A truly bad man would likely claim goodness," she said, her voice maddeningly low. "Some have tried to do so because they thought it was all I wanted to hear. Your honesty does you credit, Flynn. But do you want to know something?" She leaned forward and put a hand on his forearm; Flynn's hands clenched at her nearness. "Not all wickedness is bad," she whispered.

"Would you care to elaborate?" His voice sounded raw as Mirren withdrew, her eyes dark. "You have my full attention."

Her lips parted in a half smile that held more hunger than humor. A desire to taste her lips overcame him, and he lowered his head. But Mirren's eyes darted over his shoulder and widened. The moment crumbled like an eroding cliff. "Oh, saints, Flynn. Get down."

Flynn barely registered the figure walking towards them before Mirren grabbed him by the shirt and pulled him to the earth behind the nearest rick.

"What is it?" He sat upright, every muscle rigid, ready to fight anyone who could make her feel the need to hide, but Mirren pushed him back against the stones.

"A farmer I'd rather not speak to." Her hand still on him, her gaze was intense as she looked out over the hills. Irrational anger flared hot in Flynn's chest, competing with the heady sensation of her touch through the shirt fabric.

"What has he done?" He demanded.

"Only proposed marriage to me once every month, and he's overdue. I don't want to speak to him now."

"Don't worry. I'll dispose of the brute myself." Flynn made to stand, but Mirren flung herself across him and clamped her hands over his mouth.

"Are you daft? He's no villain!" She was shaking. Her eyes danced, silent laughter running through her body as she tried to compose her features, but that dazzling smile took over. His anger melted into something else altogether at the awareness of her body pressed against his as they lay sprawled across the earth. How easy it would be to roll her over, spread her legs, and pleasure her until she gasped and writhed and wept. His hands found and gripped her waist. He could feel the knife tucked into her skirt and moved his hand away from it, watching as the laughter fled her eyes and desire darkened them. Somehow, he had passed her test, satisfying her barrage of questioning. A shift had occurred. She'd been teasing him all morning. Perhaps it was time she got as good as she gave—or better. He smirked against her hands. *Shall I show you just how well I can play this game?*

"He is not a villain," she repeated breathlessly. "We do not hurt men like him."

Flynn kissed her hands. She withdrew them to brace herself against his shoulders, but he kept her locked against him. The blood roaring in his ears drowned the crash of the surf and the sigh of the wind.

"Then why don't you want to be his wife?"

"He isn't—he's *too* nice. Too boring. He wants a quiet little wife who will mind the fire and give him lots of children."

Flynn's grin widened. "Mirren, if there's one thing I can promise you, it's that I am not boring." Experimentally, he drew his hands down her waist to her hips. "I can be just the right kind of nice, if you want me to be."

Her breathing hitched. "And what if I prefer you wicked?"

"Do you?" Flynn's hands slid lower, gripping her through the fabric of her dress. Pausing, searching her face for any sign he should stop and finding none, he pulled her onto his lap so that she straddled one of his legs. Mirren's hips squirmed. "Shhh," he whispered, "or he'll hear you."

He curled his hands around her thighs and squeezed gently, lifting his leg just enough to press against the secret, sensitive place between her legs, the place he imagined was already wet and throbbing. Mirren's eyes fell shut and her head went back, her fingers digging into his shoulders. "Is this wicked enough?" He whispered.

When her only response was a whimper, he grinned.

"Mirren? I just want to speak to you," came a male voice nearby.

Flynn cursed under his breath. He hadn't even heard the man approach. Mirren's eyes flew open, her body tense again. His hands fisted and fell to his sides. Mirren couldn't fail to notice his frustrated arousal, but she remained on top of him. Not until the farmer left, the grass swishing in his wake, did Mirren inhale shakily, roll off of Flynn, and rise unsteadily to her feet.

Chapter 3

Mirren walked to the last rick on wobbly legs, thinking how she'd never begrudged farmer O'Neal's appearance this much before.

There was something different about Flynn, certainly. One moment she felt herself in control, and the next, he'd taken that control in a sleight of hand that defied her previous romantic encounters, only to return it again. She enjoyed this back-and-forth with him, this give and take. He had demonstrated just enough transparency to satisfy her concerns. Their interactions gave her a feeling of power, balancing between desire and caution, both thrilling and necessary.

A tingle ran through her body and left heat in its wake, reviving the unspent ache that lingered there.

She wanted him to want *her*, not just her body or what she could offer him. *It's a silly thing to want when he will probably leave the moment he gets bored.* Yet despite this, she wanted to know if she could be special to him. Her world was full of ordinary people and the overwhelming forces of the sea. She wanted to be more than merely an expected, routine acquisition picked up in the course of one's predictable life.

But it would probably never happen. And, used to steeling herself against the transient nature of life, Mirren turned her mind to more practical matters. There was the day's work to finish. Her pulsing body reminded her on no uncertain terms that it was almost over. If Flynn was still willing, they could at least have each other for one breathless, secret night.

For the rest of the day, she taught him how to replace thatch in the kelp ricks. The sun set early, as it did that time of year, and the wind kicked up and the surf battered the shore. The sky roiled with heavy grey clouds. The wind tugged at their hair and clothes. The rain began to fall, leaving dark spots on his shirt. Mirren gave the thatch one last inspection: it would hold. "Come on, let's go inside," she shouted over the storm.

They were thoroughly drenched by the time they reached the bothy and slammed the door against the downpour. Mirren's hair had fallen out of her braid and hung dripping down her back. She put more peat on the fire and watched it as it grew, aware of Flynn standing awkwardly in the corner. She hid a smile. He seemed unsure of himself, while outside by the ricks, he had known exactly what to do. Or perhaps he was waiting for her. She had sensed his hesitation the first time she'd brought him inside, though she'd also noted his gaze lingering on her bed. Her face flushed with more than the heat from the hearth.

She cleared her throat. "Come stand by the fire. You won't dry in the corner like that."

He did as commanded, which brought him closer to her and did nothing to settle her state of mind. Wet clothes clung to his spare, lean muscles. Outside, the rain fell in torrents. "You'll have to stay here," Mirren continued, biting her lip and staring into the fire. "There's no point in going to the inn in this weather."

"Mirren, you're bleeding." Flynn knelt down and touched the top of her foot, gently. Red welled from the big toe of her foot, mingling with the rapidly forming puddle. She vaguely remembered stepping on something sharp as they ran, but she was used to going barefoot, and had been focused on getting out of the rain. Now the pain rose to the forefront of her mind.

Before she could protest, Flynn pulled up one of the wooden chairs. When she remained standing, he put his hands on her hips and gently pushed her down into the chair. He crouched down and took her foot by the ankle, eliciting a shiver from her. His lashes fanned dark against his cheeks. His shoulders moved with controlled strength as he gently turned her foot from side to side. A flash of an image, of Flynn shirtless and moving over her like that, burned into her brain. But the moment he touched her again, pain shot through her foot. She sucked in a breath against a wave of dizziness as he examined the wound.

Fainting is not a good idea, she told herself. *If I faint I can't appreciate watching him.* She bit her lip hard against the lightheadedness that washed over her.

"It's deep." Flynn gestured to a piece of shell protruding from the cut, a pale point washed in blood. Glancing up, his expression softened. "This will hurt," he warned gently.

Mirren choked on an oath as he removed the shell. It was bigger than it had appeared and drew fresh blood from the gash. "Done," he said. "It needs wrapping."

"The trunk." Mirren clutched the chair as he followed her bidding, kneeling to wrap strips of old cloth around her foot.

"Wait. There's a bottle of tincture in the cupboard over there," she said, nodding at it. A few drops of the sharp-smelling remedy made her hiss. It burned like fire, but it would keep infection at bay.

"Hm." Flynn studied her face as he bandaged her foot. "You look grey as death."

"How flattering you are."

The final knot secured, he flashed a grin at her that dimpled his cheek. "You don't seem like someone easily unsettled by the sight of blood."

"You suggest I am insensitive?" Mirren was quite proud of the dry humor in her voice. "Too insensitive for a woman, maybe. But this is no life for softness."

"On the contrary." Flynn slid his hand from her foot to her ankle and stroked two fingers up her calf, igniting a spark that travelled all the way up her leg. "I believe you have the right kinds of softness. And a man who values your sensitivities might be worthy of you."

It was hard to breathe. *This is ridiculous.* Here she was blushing like an untried girl, and he knew exactly what he was doing to her. Despite her efforts to look calm, her eyelids fluttered along with the heartbeat that pulsed throughout her body. "And you," she breathed, "you believe you are worthy of me?"

"I would like to be the man who proves that you are worthy of whatever you wish."

She scoffed, but a smile played about her lips. She no longer cared to prolong this tug-of-war. She wanted it translated, spoken in the language of skin and touch.

His hand slid down to the bandage. "Will this do?" He asked, tapping the fabric with one finger, rubbing circles into the arch of her foot.

She nodded. "Those are pretty words. Do you have any more of them?"

Flynn took her other foot in one hand and traced the same path around her ankle, making her breath quicken and her heartbeat throb. "I would prefer to show you instead."

She leaned forward and kissed him quickly, teasingly, pulling back to see a muscle in his jaw twitch and his eyes flare. Flynn answered as if any distance between them would kill him. His mouth was rough and quick on hers. His tongue curled inside her and stroked. Sparks shot through her body, again and again, stoked with each movement of his tongue. His hands were at her back, gripping her now at her waist, now twisting in her loose hair. Mirren gasped as he tugged her head back and pressed a kiss to her throat, his face and teeth rough on her skin.

"Too fast?" He whispered hoarsely. "Tell me to slow down."

"No. Keep going."

She tried to protest when he broke away, but his breath feathered hot on her breast as he nuzzled her through her dress, taking her once, twice in his teeth, teasing her just enough to intensify the pleasure of his touch before moving to the other. The ache between her legs clamored for attention.

Mirren stumbled upright and tugged him away from the hearth, pausing to tug the knife free of her skirt and cast it to the floor. He followed, his eyes wild, black pools of hunger as she sat on the bed. Standing between her legs, Flynn pressed her down with one hand on her stomach, his other hand sliding her skirt down to pool around her hips. With both hands, he removed her drawers.

She gasped at the sudden rush of cool air on her intimate skin.

He groaned, his hand pausing in its way down her inner thigh, and knelt to gaze at her. "Look at you. Stunning. I can't believe I get to touch you."

Her skin quivered at the touch of his fingers, a soft, lingering stroke not quite where she wanted it. "Flynn!"

"You have the prettiest voice, Mirren. You make me weak."

A moan, part frustration, part arousal, escaped her lips as he continued teasing her.

"I wanted you as soon as I saw you," she replied, and smiled when he groaned again, pressing his face into her thigh, his motions momentarily stilled. He might make her weak with pleasure, but this was power, and she intended to use it as long as she could speak. "I've been hungry for you all day. I imagined stripping your clothes off and touching all of you. I–Flynn!"

He had touched her exactly where she wanted him. Gently at first, then with urgency, silencing her thoughts, his fingers sent all powers of speech packing with promises to return in the distant future. Pleasure swelled, tightening within her again. He tugged her closer.

"That sounds good, you taking my clothes off." His breath feathered against her neck as he leaned over her, his fingers continuing their languid exploration, the warmth of his body flush against hers. "Maybe I'll let you do that next time."

She writhed against his hand as he toyed with her. It was almost unbearable, these sensations he wrought in her. Suddenly the thread of tension snapped. Pleasure erupted with overwhelming force, making every nerve in her body sing with shaking, pulsing energy. Wave after wave pummeled her, prolonged by Flynn's touch, until she lay quivering beneath him, utterly spent and gasping for breath.

"That was so fast," she panted, deliriously sated.

"You aren't done yet." He kissed her neck softly, rubbed her arms, soothing her down from the climax. "Not if I have any say in the matter."

Chapter 4

He couldn't get enough of her. Watching her climax was the most thrilling, beautiful thing he'd ever seen. Seeing her lose control, knowing he had done that, filled him with something bordering on possessiveness. Yet he agreed silently that it had happened too quickly. Proud as he was at his skills in making her come, this was not something to rush.

He wanted to explore more of her body. To enter her again and again and feel her tremble around him. He wanted to prolong the fulfillment of her ecstasy, to draw it out for her, to watch her beg and then give her exactly what she wanted. And he throbbed with wanting her.

Mirren's languid expression brightened when he tugged his trousers off, and when she gripped his firm length, murmuring appreciatively, he almost lost it then and there.

Breathe, breathe. "Wait." Never mind that his voice was strained and his eyes shut fast. This was urgent. Mirren's hand stroked down slowly and sparks went off everywhere. *What was I going to ask?*

He forced his eyes open, Mirren's flushed face and smirking lips inflaming him further even as she withdrew her hand. Yet the question returned, urgent and necessary.

"Have you done this before?" He managed.

She nodded.

Flynn exhaled in relief. He wanted to push inside of her in one stroke. *Time, you want time! Slow! Slowly!* he reminded himself.

Mirren sat up and tugged at his shirt, trying to pull it off before he could lower himself back down.

"But I'll be naked," he grunted intelligently. "I didn't take your dress off."

"I like that." Her smile took wicked and redefined it. "Maybe I'll let you do that next time."

He had no choice but to comply. As his bare skin met the air, her hand stroked him, teasing him with the mercilessness he'd promised her. He forgot about lying down, forgot about moving, forgot about everything that wasn't her and her hands on him.

It isn't fair, something in him protested, and the rest of him bound and gagged it and kicked it out the door.

"You feel like silk, Flynn. Just as I knew you would. You could sink into me and would send us both flying, wouldn't you?"

A string of curses tripped through his mind. This was far better; this was far worse. He was more than happy for this turn of events and was furious with need for her. He was so close, so close to spilling everything; the ecstasy bordered on pain and made him wobble on his feet. With his final shred of resolve, he dove for Mirren and flipped her on top of him.

She gave a startled gasp; he felt her warm wetness settle against him as he fell back against the bed, speechless.

"Sit up," she commanded, breathless.

"You're a tyrant." And Flynn was her thrall.

"You like it that way," she whispered, nipping at his earlobe.

More curses. "So do you."

He had no choice but to obey. She teased him, dipping over him like gentle waves, and between her movements and her words, Flynn lost all control. Seizing her hips, he pulled her down onto him, thrusting deep into her in one swift movement. For a moment he could hardly breathe.

"Gods, Mirren. You're so warm. So perfect."

She went limp, whimpering against him and pressing her forehead to his shoulder as her nails dug into his skin. Her hand fisted around the silver chain at his neck. Gently he pried her hand away, pinned it to her side, and began rhythmic thrusting, pressing his hand to her lower back. He could feel her fluttering around him, could see her climb and climb again even as he reached for his own release.

"Flynn," she moaned.

"That's right." He kissed her neck, her jaw. "Let go, Mirren."

She cried out as she clamped around him, undulating and pulsing, and sent him soaring into a climax so strong he felt his soul leave his body.

He didn't know if he was silent or loud. The sensations of her body overwhelmed him even as his own floated somewhere over an endless horizon.

Shivering, Mirren relaxed against him. The press of her warm, pliant frame brought him back to earth. He lay down, gathering her to him. Even through her dress he could feel her supple languor, smell the evidence of their intimacy. *That dress will have to go next time.* She gave a contented sigh that pierced something inside of him and unleashed a hundred questions.

Wait a moment, he thought. *I felt my soul leave my body. Do I have a soul?*

His kind didn't believe they had souls. They were creatures of water, all cunning and desire and appetites. Humans had souls; they were frail creatures, and so could not keep all of themselves together for long.

Mirren adjusted herself against him and stroked a hand gently down his chest. He took her hand. Not just to stop her from taking his chain again. Even with her lying against him, he felt the need to hold onto her, as if she were an anchor. He'd never needed an anchor before.

He'd known her only a day, and yet he could tell this was something different. Something terrifyingly, unavoidably cataclysmic. He had to tell her. She had to know what he was.

But not now in this perfect moment, where his words would ruin it for both of them.

The next morning, Flynn returned to the sea.

He knew the sea far better than land. But he had never sat in a boat before, and never with a woman.

Now that he was back in his element, if he had any tension left after last night, he felt it ease from his body with each gentle lap of the waves. Out here, he was used to doing whatever he wished; swimming for endless hours, luring victims to their deaths to satisfy his appetites. Once he began interacting with humans his curiosity about them had grown, but so had his respect for them. He saw them work, fight, sing, laugh, and harden themselves to the difficulties of life. The times he'd taken his human shape and wandered amongst them had proven most informative.

And then there was Mirren.

She sat in the other end of the tiny boat as he rowed, her injured foot poking out beneath her skirts, where the bandage showed a dull patch of brownish red. The tincture, a strange human remedy, seemed to be helping her. For that he was grateful.

Gratitude, protectiveness, possessiveness, fear–these human emotions were wearing on him, getting under his skin. He found the experience both exhausting and exhilarating. His other senses were weakened in this human form, otherwise he'd be out of his mind, a living whirlpool on land. Somehow he didn't miss the old sensations when he was with Mirren. As odd as this experience was, he never wanted to lose this human form, as long as it allowed him to be close to her.

I'm sitting in a boat with her, and she's teaching me how to use a net.

He'd finally done it. He'd stepped out of the observer's role and ventured into her world, and found, to his utter astonishment and delight, that she wanted him.

She wanted me! He felt like shouting. *She enjoyed my...company.* He grinned.

They threw out the net and secured it amidst the gentle rocking of the waves. He couldn't interpret Mirren's expression as she looked out at the water, whether she was content or intent on something he couldn't identify.

"You must swim frequently," he said.

Mirren shot him a bemused glance. "Why would I do that?"

"Too cold?" Ah, yes. It was cold this time of year for humans. That must be why, despite her proximity to water, he'd never seen her swimming in the past. "In the summer, then," he said, thinking the waters must be marginally warmer when the days were longer and the sky less often clouded.

"I don't know how," she said, as if it were the most obvious thing in the world.

Flynn's eyes widened. Surprise, incredulity: there was another human emotion he was unused to. "You can't swim? But that's impractical. How can you not swim if you are surrounded by water?"

"Most of us never learn," she said.

"What if your boat capsizes?"

"We live and die by the sea, Flynn. It's part of life."

"No. Not anymore." He could do this for her. How could she so easily accept the fragility of her life, as if losing it were nothing? He couldn't allow it, not when he could do something for her benefit. "I'll teach you to swim. Then you won't have to die by it."

"I don't know." She frowned at the water. Was she afraid? It would make sense. The fleeting terror of previous victims flitted across Flynn's mind. Yes, humans were afraid of the deep water where they couldn't breathe or see, where creatures like him lurked.

His solution meant staying with her for much longer than a day. Would she have him?

"What do you say this, Mirren. I'll teach you how to swim in the summer."

Her smile was tentative. "Very well. The summer, then."

Mirren undressed slowly. They'd finished the day's work and had eaten a late meal, and now she was preparing for bed. As if they'd always done this together. When she stood in her undergarments, he couldn't wait any longer and took hold of her, spun her around, and kissed her.

"I promised you I'd undress." Her protestation slipped out between kisses.

"You said you'd let me undress you. There is a difference."

Her dark hair was already tousled, spilling over her shoulders. Her lips were red, her eyes heavy.

He knelt down and took the hem of her shift, sliding it up her thighs until he reached her bare hips and exposed her center. Flynn bit back a groan at the sight. She shifted, her hands clutching his shoulders, and he knew he'd do better to wait than to touch her, to dip his finger inside her as he wanted. Prolong both their torment to heighten their relief. "I haven't had the pleasure of seeing your breasts yet." His thumbs brushed her belly, the base of her breasts, and he had to pause, his shoulders going tense and his hands tightening on the fabric as Mirren's breath quickened.

"Why have you stopped?" Came her low, teasing voice.

He pulled the gown over her head and tossed it aside, then stepped back to stare in undisguised admiration.

Her breasts were small and round. A freckle adorned the skin between them. She was slim, not voluptuous or what some might call well-formed, yet to him she was perfect. And as stunning as she was, he found his gaze landing on her smirk, the way her eyes invited and challenged him at once.

"And now what?" she said.

"Now, I want to wipe that smile off your face and make you breathless in my arms." He scooped her up and put her on the bed. In bending forward, he felt the chain slip from his shirt. Mirren tugged his shirt off and discarded it. Then she gripped the chain, trying to find the clasp, causing his thoughts to skip.

"Take it off?" She asked. A faint, questioning smile was on her lips, the haze of arousal leaving her eyes. *No,* he thought. *Not now.*

He kissed her fiercely, startling a whimper from her, and pressed her hands against the bed with one of his. He trailed kisses down her breasts, her belly, and into her center, releasing her hands as he went.

Mirren fumbled onto her elbows, watching him through fluttering eyelids, faint surprise on her face.

"Have you done this before?" He murmured, and was gratified to see her shudder with the humming of his voice against her skin.

"No. Have you?"

In reply, he grinned, reaching up to caress her breast. Mirren's head fell back, and, satisfied that his answer satisfied her, continued his slow, sensuous exploration. He could feel her flutter around his tongue.

"Flynn," she moaned. Her breath hitched.

"What is it?" He said, grinning. "Tell me in that pretty voice of yours."

Her eyes flared, her expression a mix of irritation and arousal. Flynn hummed again, ruthlessly pleasuring her, the flutterings growing stronger as she writhed. "Tell me, Mirren."

Her hand caught his shoulder and tugged at him. "I want you."

Flynn rose from the floor, his own breath coming fast as he stared down at her desperate form, her arched back and legs spread for him. *You're so ready for me.*

He plunged inside of her, pressing her against the bed with his hand spread on her chest, her eyes widening before she arched and cried out, tightening and squeezing around him. He reached his own climax only after he had brought her to the peak twice more, every part of him hungry for her.

The feel of her skin on his was better than the caress of waves. Her contented sighs feathered on his chest. And beneath all this calm, this otherworldly bliss, there hovered a growing fear.

Pleasuring and plundering her didn't sate his feelings for her. If anything, their intensity increased. He wanted to be with Mirren indefinitely. But what if he couldn't be human enough for her? Even more unsettling, what if he could? Was it even possible to become more human? The thought haunted him. And with that, came another realization.

He was a monster. Not just a shifter who could pass from one form and one life to another. As a monster, he could never be worthy of her. He wanted to hide away, to tuck his nature deep inside and forget it ever existed. Yet how could he be worthy of her if he kept her from the truth?

"Why don't you take it off?"

He'd thought she was asleep, but Mirren's fingers stroked the fine chain, turning it as if trying to catch the firelight on it.

He swallowed. "It's important."

"Was it from someone?"

He paused. "In a way." His father, long ago, had given it to him, a rite of passage he'd never thought to be so grateful for and conflicted over. It had allowed him to find her. It had allowed so many questions into his life, and Mirren was the biggest question of all.

She dropped the chain and sighed, nestling against him so that her curls tickled his nose. He let out a sigh of his own.

"Tell me about it someday."

"Maybe—"

"You know if you hem and haw, you'll only make me more curious." She laughed softly, her voice drowsy and content. Flynn doubted Mirren was one to forget things.

He tightened his arms around her. "I promise."

It was the first time in his life he had ever been terrified.

This is going to be terrible, isn't it?

Chapter 5

Weeks passed. Winter changed to spring in small island ways, as Mirren knew it would. Flynn stayed. She hadn't expected that.

They spent their days working. Their nights, tangled in a tide of pleasure. The pull between them was like the ocean: a give and take, sometimes turbulent, infrequently calm, a thing of haunting beauty and death and life. Mirren sometimes wondered if she was lost in him or found. She could never bring herself to press too much for an answer.

As the days warmed incrementally, she found Flynn looking out at sea more and more and began to feel unsettled by it. They said nothing about his unknown past. She believed he had no one waiting for him and didn't care about anything else. But did he have somewhere he needed to be? Or did he grow restless, for other horizons or other people?

He was no scholar, but few islanders learned to read. When she taught him fishing and other skills he learned easily, but had no prior experience with them. She wondered more and more of his life before they'd met and was afraid to ask him, as if it would break whatever fragile spell held them together. The romance of mystery held her in too tight a grip. But there was a mystery surrounding his necklace, too. Of this she felt certain, and it gnawed on her more every day.

One day the weather was fair enough that she took him up to the patch of land that would soon be her garden. There was no sign of farmer O'Neal on the hills, or of anyone else. Mirren spread stories that she'd married Flynn in secret so that the villagers, including O'Neal, would leave her alone. They did, though they sometimes watched the two of them with suspicion when they visited the village. But that day the grasses waved beneath a pale blue sky half covered in white clouds, and with a sly look, she pulled Flynn to the earth. They kissed ravenously, hungrily, as if they hadn't exhausted one another the night before, as if she would never see him again. She ached for him, needed him in a way that felt startlingly different. His face contorted in pleasure as she straddled him, coaxing and guiding, until he was inside of her, filling her perfectly.

They rocked in rhythm, groaning. His fingers dug into her thighs. Her motions were desperate, graceless, but so was she, seeking something she dreaded and desired.

"Tell me about the necklace," she said, then gasped as he found an especially sensitive place. Flynn gripped her arms and thrust faster. Her head fell back. She bit her tongue to keep from crying out. "You promised," she moaned. "Tell me."

"Not now." Flynn took hold of her waist and rolled over, pinning her beneath him, turning her face with one hand to make her look at him. His eyes were ablaze. "Please, Mirren."

"You always—say—that." She'd asked him twice before. She was done waiting. But her body responded the way it always did to him. Sensation took over and sent thoughts far away as a wave pummeled her over and over again, leaving her weak and floating beneath his hot, strong body. She watched him reach his own climax. His hair brushed her face, his features contorted, and he strained within her. He was beautiful in his abandon, in this intimate exchange of power where they both lost and they both won. She studied every line of his face and found what she always did—something hidden in his features, something he withheld from her. Mirren wanted all of him.

She stroked his back as they lay together, his body half over hers, and she watched the clouds fly overhead as his panting turned to slow, rhythmic breaths.

Flynn slept.

Her hand found the chain at his neck. Why was his secret necessary? Was it terrible? Was *he* terrible?

She unclasped it. Slender metal, warm from Flynn's skin, pooled in her hand. The charm looked like a tiny horse.

Flynn shuddered and woke.

"Mirren," he cried. "Mirren! What have you done?"

He was crushing her, shaking violently. Frightening, inhuman sounds emanated from his naked chest, which grew barrel-like in shape and size. Mirren scrambled away with a cry of fear and could not look away, uncomprehending.

Within minutes, there was no Flynn.

The creature that stood before her wasn't human. Silver hair flowed down the long, grey neck. Four long, powerful legs ended in hooves. Sea grey eyes became large, swirling pools of darkness.

Mirren stared, transfixed in horror. One word echoed in her mind, yet she couldn't comprehend it anymore than she could comprehend what– who–stood before her.

The beast regarded her with its eerie eyes. Its sides heaved; nostrils flared, snorted. It stepped towards her.

"No!" She cried. "Get away with you!"

The creature swayed from side to side as Mirren shouted at it. Then with a whinny and a toss of its neck, the creature rose up on hind legs to paw at the air before turning and running towards the beach, its mane and tail flowing.

Mirren bolted for home.

The shoreline taunted her when it came into view, calm, temperate, and steady, everything she was not. There was no sign of anyone else. She slammed the door behind her and stood, panting, before the red-ember hearth, in the space she had shared with Flynn, in a space that felt as distant and strange as he did.

What were the last few weeks, but a storm waiting to break? What was Flynn, but a total stranger?

A kelpie, her harried mind told her. *Flynn is a kelpie.*

Mirren worked in a frenzy, trying to put everything from her mind over the next few days. The bothy felt larger without him. She could almost forget him during the day. Or at least, pretend that she could. But night still came on, and with it, the end of the day's work, the end of her attempted distraction, and the transformation on the hills returned to her harried mind in a roar.

His human shape breaking, shattered, gone.

Her thoughts stumbled and disappeared. She ached for him, missed him in her bed, in her body. His presence had become a constant. Far beneath her fears that he would leave, she had begun to expect that he would stay, an undercurrent of longing for him that went beyond rationality.

It is impossible now. No more.

She had lived alone before, and she would do it again. There was always work to keep her occupied and to give her purpose. She would work him from her mind, her body, her heart. She would harden her heart, which balked at the idea like a stubborn kel–horse–balking at a bridle. She would tell the villagers her husband drowned at sea. If she ever saw him again, she'd drown him herself–never mind that these encounters usually resulted in the opposite outcome for those involved.

Had Flynn ever really existed? Was the man who had shared her bed nothing more than a lie? The ache in her chest grew. The man who had held her, pleasured her senseless, worked alongside her for weeks? He'd made her life not just bearable, but colorful, vibrant. She thought she'd found purpose in work, but life held meaning with Flynn. Had she loved something no more substantial than sea foam?

No, she told herself, *I didn't love him. I don't.* But her heart whispered, *I'm afraid you do.*

She stumbled out of bed one morning, having slept little. She told herself this morning would be different. *Time for an ordinary day!* Sang her mind, with all the vigor of the happily deluded.

When she went outside, on the beach stood a grey horse with a silver mane. *Fuck,* said her mind, and delusion slid away like sand.

He'd appeared every morning for the past two weeks. Since talking to him had gotten her into trouble in the first place, she had ignored him. *No reason to stop now.* She stormed off to start the day's business in a cool and composed manner that did not bely her anger and hurt, not at all.

Flynn–the kelpie–kept his distance all morning, but he was there. This, too, was routine. *You could try to scare him away*, said a part of her. *Shut up,* said another. *I would if I needed to.*

She was breaking up the earth in her garden today for planting turnips. The soil wasn't terribly forgiving, but she welcomed the work. The ache in her muscles would be a welcome distraction from other aches, some in her body and some in her heart, both for wanting him.

A presence stood nearby. Mirren looked up from her work and gasped, then frowned.

"What do you want?" She snapped.

He stood at the edge of her garden, quiet as a ghost, two arms' breadths away yet unnervingly close. She did not know much about horses, but she had to admit that the kelpie was truly beautiful. For a moment his beauty took her breath away. His coat gleamed and he looked like everything from a story, the calm of the sea before a storm. He should have been terrifying. Somehow, not even his eyes frightened her anymore. Something hung from his mouth. For a moment her stomach lurched and she wondered if he'd caught some poor soul. Had he brought the tattered, gory remains to her like some kind of terrible offering?

But on closer inspection, the thing in the monster's mouth was slender and brown and not at all human-like. Lowering his head, the kelpie dropped it to the ground, turned, and walked away. Mirren waited for him to vanish over the crest of the hill before tentatively studying the object half-hidden in tall grass.

The something was a bridle.

She was working at her garden, the silver horse charm lying against her skin, when the kelpie approached her the next day. His head low, he watched her through long lashes with eyes that seemed–sad? contrite? She snorted at the thought, sounding like a horse herself, and his ears flicked forward.

"Have you come to help me?" she asked.

The kelpie ducked his head. Mirren touched the chain at her neck. "Do you want this back? You could take it. Steal it like I did. Bite my head off. Tear me apart, drag me into the ocean. Is that what you were doing, Flynn? Biding your time until you could kill me?"

The kelpie looked at her with his uncanny gaze.

Mirren tossed her bag of seeds to the ground. Like any islander, she'd grown up with the tales of kelpies: monsters who lured victims close with their equine beauty, only to drown and devour those foolish enough to touch them. Creatures of the tempestuous, primal waters.

Yet she'd done her fair share of touching him. Slept beside him, worked beside him. He'd had any number of chances to destroy her. And he hadn't.

"Well, maybe you'd rather be in your true form. Maybe you got tired of being a man. I saw you watching the sea."

Flynn nudged the plow, making the heavy, burdensome thing look tiny. Mirren had found it leaning up against the bothy this morning. She'd dragged it up here herself, and it seemed a pity to waste the tool and the help now.

As Mirren hitched him to the plow, she wasn't sure if she was relieved or sad that Flynn couldn't answer her.

Chapter 6

The plowing didn't take him long. The relief Flynn felt at being near her again was indescribable. He wanted to take his human form back and speak with her, hold her. But Mirren needed to see him as he truly was. If he wasn't trustworthy as a kelpie, how would he ever be trustworthy as a man?

Though his transformation had been a shock, it was also a relief. The agony over his secret had grown unbearable. He knew he was a coward for it, but he was grateful to her for stripping him of the choice between living a continued lie or revealing his true self.

He couldn't help with the planting, but he kept her company the next morning when she did so. The morning after that, he met her outside the bothy where she sat amidst the grass, staring out at the waves in an uncharacteristically listless pose. Flynn snorted a soft greeting.

She glanced at him. "Still here?" The anger in her voice had dulled, leaving it sad. It pierced something in Flynn's kelpie chest. Mirren, wrapped in her shawl, offered him a brief smile before returning her gaze to the sea.

"I knew you were too good to be real," she said softly. She poked her bare foot out and curled it into the sand. Her scar was so pale, he wouldn't have known to look for it if he hadn't been there to bind it up that first night in her bothy. "You were something out of a dream. Now my life feels like nothing. Not even a nightmare. It's a little ridiculous."

She attempted a carefree tone on those last words, but they fell like brittle glass. Flynn ached to comfort her. He wanted so much to wrap her in his arms and smell her clean, soapy scent tinged with salt, to tell her he was still here, and that he would never leave her. He'd forsaken his violent kelpie ways ever since he met her. Even before he'd stepped out of the sea, naked as a newborn and eager to be in her presence, he'd known he could never go back to killing humans. It was as true now as it had been then.

Mirren dug into her neckline and pulled out the silver horse on its chain, watching it dance in the early light. She glanced at Flynn. "Will you take it?"

Instinctively, he pulled back. He was still a kelpie. Could she ever accept him, now that she knew what he was? He wasn't ready to face her as a man. Not until he'd proven himself to her.

Sighing, she replaced the chain around her own neck.

"Then teach me how to ride. I've never ridden a horse."

Mirren's unexpected command sent a sharp jolt through him, like a hidden shell burrowing into a wound. Ride him? *Have you lost your senses, Mirren?* He wasn't a horse, he was a kelpie. He tried to put her off with a teasing chuckle, forgetting that he could only snort and whinny.

She cocked an eyebrow at him, her expression dangerously sharp. "Not 'ride you' like that. Don't put me off trying to be funny."

Flynn backed up when she stood, nostrils flaring, but Mirren held out a gentle hand.

"Are you afraid?"

Was he? Of course he was. Afraid of what? Of forgetting everything he'd learned as a human? That he'd turn wild and hurt her, drown her, kill her?

"Flynn." Understanding dawned in her eyes. Her face softened. She remained still, letting her hand drop. "Please. Can you do this for me?"

She was offering him a chance to prove himself, the very chance he longed for. She wanted to know if she could trust him. Was he trustworthy enough for her?

I don't know. I want to be.

How can I refuse you, when you ask like that?

Mirren was a fast learner. She climbed on his back easily enough, clinging to him tightly and reminding him of all the nights he'd spent happily trapped between her legs. He didn't feel the same desire for her in kelpie form that he felt in human form. But it was pure delight, dangerous and sweet and tumultuous, to feel her slim weight on his back, to feel her hands fisting his mane and to hear her quickened breath as he walked slowly.

He continued walking for some time, threading through the island's hills near her bothy. The sole time Mirren fell off and landed on a tussock, she clambered to her feet, laughing, before Flynn could even be alarmed. Once she had remained on his back for some time and he felt her ease slightly, Flynn began to canter. When she urged him on, murmuring low in his ear, he broke into a gallop.

Mirren's excited laughter broke through the sough of wind in the grass. She leaned closer to him, finding the rhythm easily as she had during their nights wrapped in each other's arms. Pride glowed in Flynn's chest. *That's my Mirren. How well you learn.*

They rode for hours. Mirren learned to steer him, to communicate without words when she wanted to gallop or slow to a walk or dismount. He could feel her own pride mirrored in his. Then she steered him away from the hills. The sea came into view and Flynn's elation twisted. *She wouldn't. Would she?*

She was. She was steering him towards the water. He could not stop, but his thoughts galloped.

What if my possessiveness towards her is no better than a kelpie's lusts? What if the sea brings my past nature back? What if I am no better in human form than in my true form? I may have traded my kelpie appetites for human ones, but what if I destroy her all the same? He tossed his mane and whinnied, snorting and balking his panic.

"Shhh, Flynn. It's all right." Mirren leaned over his neck, stroking him, hugging him. "I'm here. I'm here." It was no use, though. His body reared once, backing away from the surf. Mirren slid from his back and landed expertly at his side, taking his face in her hands. His breath blew the hair back from her face. "I'm sorry, Flynn. I didn't think. I didn't know it would frighten you."

She flung her arms around his neck, and suddenly all was well. "I'm sorry," she whispered, over and over again, until he ached again to comfort her, his own fears a speck on the horizon rather than a tidal wave. "I never should have taken your necklace."

My lovely, dearest Mirren, there is nothing left to forgive.

"Come back to me, Flynn," she whispered. He couldn't see her, pressed against his neck as she was, but the words shifted something inside of him. The necklace swung into view as Mirren stepped back, holding it out to him. "Teach me to swim like you promised," she said. "I need to see you. Come back to me."

Suddenly, he knew he could. She had embraced him in his original form. He wanted to take his true form, the one where he felt most himself.

He lowered his head towards the necklace. Mirren's surprised murmur echoed in his ears as the chain stretched in her hands, fitting easily round his equine neck, and he felt the cool, thin strand of metal against his skin. The world shifted and cracked. His bones crumbled and regrew in one searing, shattering moment. He stood before her as a man, naked and trembling like a newborn colt with the aftereffects of transformation. The full return of his human emotions punched him in the gut with the strength of a hundred fists.

Why is this so damned awful? He wondered, grimacing. *Ah, yes. The last time you chose transformation, you were in the sea.*

Before Mirren had taken his necklace, he hadn't allowed himself to dwell on how much he could lose. Now, everything he wanted stood before him, face-to-face once more. Instead of losing her, she had embraced him. All his human desires came rushing back. And with them, a profound and unwavering certainty.

Mirren's wide-eyed stare darted up and down his form, her throat bobbing.

"I'd forgotten about your clothes," she said, and cleared her throat. "Do you want them?"

"They'll weigh me down in the water." His voice was husky with disuse. "Unless you'd rather I wore them."

Mirren hesitated briefly, biting her lip. Then she stripped down to her bare skin, her wide eyes never leaving his face. Not, that is, until the pleasure of seeing her naked became obvious in his own body, drawing her gaze down.

"People will talk if they see you," he managed. A smile, more shy than sly, twisted her pretty mouth. With a toss of her hair she walked into the surf, leaving Flynn to follow.

If she is a tide, I have already drowned, and I give myself wholly to her.

She gasped when the water hit her knees. Her arms thrown out, every line of her body tense, she was trying bravely to keep from looking nervous, and meanwhile Flynn was reminded that the cold water did nothing to dampen his desire.

But Mirren was shivering violently, her skin prickling with the cold. The sky was fading to pale twilight.

"Would you rather wait?" he asked, coming to stand at her side and refraining from taking her in his arms to warm her. *I'd do more than that if I could. But she doesn't need that now.* "The sea will be here tomorrow."

She shook her head. "I want to do this. No more waiting."

Even as she plunged ahead with the grace of a sea bird on land, Flynn couldn't help admiring her and the slight curves of her body that tightened and relaxed with each effort. The waves curled silver and green towards them, filling the air with their briny tang. Mirren yelped as one splashed against her and sent spray into her face. Flynn caught up to her easily. He wasn't much taller than she was, but even in his human form the steadily growing waves shocked him less, and he didn't mind the dousing. He'd be willing to put up with a lot more discomfort if it meant staying with her in this moment. Yet still Mirren fought to remain calm, her shoulders tight as she forged ahead.

"The floor drops just ahead," he warned. "Take my hand, Mirren."

She did so, keeping her eyes fixed on the darkening horizon. Flynn couldn't help the smile that broke across his face; she was touching him again, without hesitation, and it felt so right and true. "Here it is," he said, and the next moment he was treading water, held in the water's rocking embrace, carefully bringing her out with him.

Mirren made a panicked sound and bobbed like an apple, the water rising to her neck. "It's all right," he soothed, taking both her hands, then her waist, holding her steady as she flailed, ignoring how his body responded to her proximity. "I won't let you go under."

"I can't, Flynn! It's too deep!"

"Yes, you can. Just tread with your feet and let the waves carry you. It's like walking."

Mirren gripped his arms so tightly her nails dug into his skin, her breathing erratic and shallow, her legs kicking out uselessly. Flynn turned to the side and narrowly avoided an ill-placed knee to the groin. That, at least, helped his nether regions calm down a little.

"Mirren," he grunted, "I'm not letting go."

She stopped thrashing at once, her eyes fixed on the sliver of water lapping between them.

"I'm not letting go," he repeated. *Mirren, I'll do anything not to fail you.* "I'm not letting go."

He continued murmuring gently until her shoulders dropped and her shallow breaths became slower, her movements less frantic. As good as it felt to hold her, he knew better than to remain still too long. Once Mirren relaxed into the rhythm of the waves, he swam them out to where they rose higher, easing her through each one until she anticipated and rode the undulations without resistance.

"Better?"

She nodded vigorously, her teeth chattering as she spoke. "So I can float, that isn't swimming. Teach me how to swim now."

"You have to push out with your arms and kick out with your legs." He demonstrated with one arm while keeping the other around her waist, then moved to give her space to practice, still holding onto her. As with riding, it didn't take Mirren long to learn. Flynn, who had struggled to learn how to fish with a net and bake bread and a number of other mundane human activities, would have found her efficiency irritating were he not so thrilled to be with her. She even pushed his arms away and swam in a circle on her own, her face brightening as she rose and dipped with the waves.

When a larger wave rolled towards them, her confidence slipped again. "I can't," she said, panic widening her eyes, her limbs flailing again.

"Yes, you can. We'll ride it together." Flynn acted almost on instinct. He pulled her against his chest, wrapping her in his arms and treading for both of them as the wave pushed them up, up, up, and gently bore them back down. Mirren shrieked and held onto him, but he felt the lessening of tension in her body, and the shriek bordered on laughter. "You see?" He murmured. "We made it through."

She relaxed against him. They found a rhythm with their legs so as not to kick each other while she remained in his arms. His throat closed, his eyes closed, and the expansive place in his chest opened even more. He inhaled her scent. This was perfect. She was perfect. How was she so perfect? He wanted this moment to last forever. Although he was grateful for the small space between them, as his body clearly wanted a lot more than just to hold her. The bowl of the sky turned deepest blue shot with pinpricks of light, leaving the water dark and glimmering in starlight.

"Is this you?" she said, a whisper so small it almost drowned in the waves. "Is Flynn real?"

"This is real," he replied, without hesitation. "You make me real."

She withdrew to search his face. "What does that mean?" Fear flashed across her features. "Do you want to remain a kelpie? If you do, I will let you go."

"No." By the depths, the last thing he wanted was to lose her. *Never again.*

"Do you mean, you expect me to keep you human? Help me understand, Flynn."

He complied eagerly. "When we met, you asked if I'd lost something. I'd lost myself. I wasn't sure who I was. But because of you, I know who I am. I want to live as a human. But I'm scared,

Mirren." He leaned his forehead against hers, fearing to look into her eyes, feeling suddenly cold and Mirren was the only warmth he could sense in the world. "I want you so much it frightens me. I can't hurt you again."

"Oh, Flynn." Her voice was unbearably tender. "Perhaps our kinds have more in common than you think. We both can be possessive and destructive, carried away by our lusts." She inhaled slowly. "I never wanted to ask where you'd come from because I feared you would disappear. But it's you I love, Flynn, all of you. And it's your life. You cannot choose how you will live for my sake alone."

Something settled into place with her words. "Whatever my soul is made of, it is set alight by the very existence of the woman I love. *Is mise mo anam.*" Flynn pulled her close, feeling as if every fiber of his being would burst with happiness as a sympathetic tremor ran through her lithe body. "What if I choose a life with you? Will you let me live by your side, Mirren?"

In response, she kissed him.

Chapter 7

There was something good about being held by Flynn in the sea. It was here, rocked by the vast ocean depths, that he was his truest self. The self Mirren had been afraid to behold, yet had longed for all the same.

It had come to her that very morning, looking out across the waves. She was ready to speak to him. Needed to speak to him, even though it frightened her to think of what he might say, that he might resent her for breaking his trust. She had wanted him to be different from the men of the island with their predictable, settled lives, and different he certainly was. Flynn must have refused the necklace before because he was afraid. As scared as she was, even, that what they had was nothing but a fantasy which could not withstand the harsh gaze of reality.

If he is afraid to come to me as a human, I must go to Flynn the kelpie.

Now, in his arms once again, everything felt right and true and whole, so much so that she couldn't put it into words, and instead kissed him with everything she had. Mirren giggled against his mouth at the feel of him hard and smooth against her hip.

"I love you, Flynn." They were playful together, bright. She could be soft with him and safe, and he wouldn't try to file down her edges. She couldn't find words to explain this and gave up trying when his hands slid down her hips. He rested his head on her shoulder.

"I love you. I love you with all that I am. I want to show you and I can't do it here." Flynn pressed a soft kiss to her neck, sending shivers up her spine that had nothing to do with the cold water. "Please let me show you, Mirren."

If anyone saw them run naked up the beach, Mirren neither noticed nor cared. The secrecy of the little bothy enveloped them. There was no fire in the hearth; she didn't care about that, either. She pressed him down on the bed and lay atop him, his eyes flaring with a hunger that mirrored her own. She kissed his jaw, his neck, and finally, softly, the chain on his chest.

"I love you, Flynn." The words spilled from her with an urgency she could not deny.

He shuddered beneath her as she straddled him. He tried to roll her over, but she put a gentle hand to his chest.

"Wait. Will you let me do this for you?"

He nodded, and Mirren smiled. His eyes fell shut and a groan escaped Flynn's lips when she touched him with well-practiced strokes. Their breath mingled. She felt his heart beating faster to match her own, could see him climb and climb.

He was completely under her command. She reveled in it. She wanted to share it.

"Come inside me," she whispered in his ear, and he gripped her hips as she enveloped him in one movement that drew a string of curses from her lover.

"You fit me so perfectly," she panted, remaining still, savoring the fullness of him, the hard, smooth weight of him inside her body. "Do you want this to last?"

Flynn grunted, his face contorting in agonized pleasure. "I don't know if I can."

She began rocking, but he stopped her roughly. "Wait. Please."

He felt so good inside her that stopping was the last thing she wanted, but Mirren did as he asked. She kept her hips still while kissing him deeply, lingering at his mouth while his hands trailed sensation across her skin. As long as she didn't move, he wouldn't find the place deep inside her that drove her over the edge. But her body ached to move.

"Do you still want to wait?" She pulled back and sat up slowly. The change in position was enough to drive a frenzied expression across Flynn's face. She laughed softly. "Haven't we waited long enough?"

"Do what you want," Flynn said roughly. "I'm yours. All of me." He reached up to brush his thumbs across her breasts, sending a jolt of pleasure deep into her core. Holding her ribcage, he repeated the motion with increasing pressure until Mirren couldn't help rocking against him, drawing him further in with each motion. She fell forward, bracing on either side of Flynn's head, and let him pull her hips. She was a frenzy of need, climbing her own pleasure with every thrust, watching him do the same. With the last of her quickly-receding faculties of speech, she administered all of her skills, whispering words that pulled him into the very depths of pleasure.

He strained against her, groaning her name, squeezing her hips so hard she might have bruises. Mirren didn't care, not when he reached an especially sensitive spot at the same time and sent her flying through a rapture of pleasure so sudden that she was nothing more than every pulsing, singing nerve in her body.

When at last she floated down to earth, Flynn's arms were tight around her, moving her gently so that she rested her head on his chest. They both laughed at his fumbling attempts to grasp hold of the blanket. When he managed to pull it over their warm, heavy bodies, Mirren sighed and snuggled closer.

"I don't think I can walk," he said. "I don't want to leave this bed. Or you."

Mirren smiled sleepily. "Neither do I. Oh, I do love you, Flynn."

Flynn's breath escaped in a short exhale, his cheek dimpling with an answering smile. "I meant what I said, too." His hand found hers and looped the chain across her fingers. "I want to be with you, as long as I live. Will you have me?"

Mirren, remembering his tears in the ocean, understood his need for reassurance.

She drew the silver horse charm to her lips and kissed it. Then she placed it back on Flynn's chest, stroking the dusting of hair. "I'll have you and keep you. All of you." Then for additional reassurance she kissed him, tenderly, deeply, pouring everything her words couldn't say into the kiss. *I do believe I could ride him again*, her inner voice said, and her drowsy body replied, *just give me a few minutes and I will.*

She propped herself up on an elbow, watching his face turn serious as he posed a question.

"Should we get married, truly? Have a real human ceremony and everything?"

"To tell the whole world we belong to each other? I believe we could." She wanted to do it now.

Not quite yet, said her body, *we have things to do. Specifically, things to do with him.* And she moved to lie across him again, to tease a smile from him, and to lose and find herself in the pleasure they created, wild and untamed as the sea and intimate as shared secrets in the night.

THE END

Thank You

There is a folktale from the isle of Barra about a kelpie who takes a human form to woo the woman he has fallen in love with. Others say he was a water horse. Either way, I am indebted to whoever first imagined such a romantic tale about such a creature. As far as I know, the liberty of making the sea Flynn's first home is mine, since we all know kelpies live in fresh water. The ocean just seemed to suit him. Then again, I imagine there are as many variations of this tale as there are tellers of it, so maybe it isn't that unique at all.

Now that I start writing my personal thank you's, I'm overwhelmed with the kindness of everyone who helped bring this story to life. Thank you to Thea Masen for reading early drafts of Mirren and Flynn's story. I probably wouldn't be publishing sexy stories without your inspiration, help, and wise writerly insights.

Thank you to Stephanie Escobar for reading this book, for your heart-warming enthusiasm which carried me through edits, and for helping to flesh out these characters.

Missy Miller, Lindsey Shipley, Rolexia Pittman, Fiona Thomson, Daphka Imbert, Kimberly Patton, Andie @she.reads2escape, Hester Fox, Alyssa Subsinsky, Ragne, Aakanksha, Natalie Hitchcox, Piper Hawthorne, Jocelyn @mama.reads.alot, Jess @jess.reads.everything,

Kim Uyehara, Anik Bellefleur, Blanca Aguilar, Mckayla Price, Chelsea @willtherebedragons, and Elle @booksandnthings–your support blows me away. (And if I misspelled any of your names, I apologize!)

And thank you to *you*, for reading this story. I'm so glad we've crossed paths.

More from Riona Beck

The Waterlore Romance series:

Crystalline
Ella and Rodan~ crumbling English manor
~virgin/'playboy' vibes
~hints of Cinderella & The Frog Prince
~seductive water spirit who refuses to seduce her

Available in ebook and paperback

The Waterlore Romance series is a collection of short, sweet, and steamy romance inspired by European folklore, fairy tales, and the author's obsession with bodies (of water). They can be read in any order. *More TBA!*

About the Author

Riona Beck used to hate romance novels, until she realized that the real problems were patriarchy and purity culture. Among others...

When Riona began to see that her hang-ups around this particular genre were protective measures she no longer needed, she discovered how much she actually liked kissy, sexy books. She even decided to start writing and publishing romance stories for real.

While she loves a good plot and adores character friendships, and is constantly analyzing the ways in which the world of romance sometimes upholds harmful narratives, you can always find her working on her next feel-good, serotonin-delivering story full of banter, chemistry, and kissing. And yes, sex.

You can follow Riona on Instagram: @rionabeckromance

Milton Keynes UK
Ingram Content Group UK Ltd.
UKHW020009061124
450708UK00001B/61